YASMIN

The Explorer

written by
SAADIA FARUQI

illustrated by
HATEM ALY

To Mariam for inspiring me, and
Mubashir for helping me find the
right words —S.F.

To my sister, Eman, and her amazing
girls, Jana and Kenzi —H.A.

Raintree is an imprint of Capstone Global Library Limited, a company
incorporated in England and Wales having its registered office at
264 Banbury Road, Oxford, OX2 7DY – Registered company number:
6695582

www.raintree.co.uk
myorders@raintree.co.uk

Text © 2019 Saadia Faruqi
Illustrations © 2019 Picture Window Books

Edited by Kristen Mohn
Designed by Aruna Rangarajan
Originated by Capstone Global Library Ltd
Printed and bound in India

ISBN 978 1 4747 6556 5
22 21 20 19 18
10 9 8 7 6 5 4 3 2 1

British Library Cataloguing in Publication Data
A full catalogue record for this book is available from the British
Library.

Acknowledgements
We would like to thank the following for permission to reproduce
design elements: Shutterstock: Art and Fashion, rangsan paidaen.

TABLE OF CONTENTS

CHAPTER 1

Ancient maps

One afternoon Yasmin sat reading with Baba.

"A long time ago, explorers used big paper maps to find their way," Baba said.

"What's an explorer?" asked Yasmin.

"Someone who discovers new places. An adventurer," Baba said.

Yasmin looked at the maps in Baba's book. There were straight roads and curvy roads. There were lakes and rivers and forests.

"I want to be an explorer!" she said.

"Well, then, the first thing you'll need is a map," Baba replied.

Yasmin clapped her hands.
"I'll make a map of our
neighbourhood."

"Good idea," Baba said.

Yasmin found crayons and
paper.

She drew their house. Down
the street was the farmers' market.
Near that was the park.

"This is excellent, jaan!" Baba

said, using his pet name for her.

Soon Mama came in.

"Yasmin, I'm going to the farmers' market. Would you like to come with me?"

Yasmin jumped up. "Yes! It will be an exploration!" She could hardly wait as Mama got her hijab and handbag.

"Don't forget your map!" Baba said. "Every explorer needs a map."

CHAPTER 2

The farmers' market

Mama and Yasmin walked down the street to the farmers' market. The air was fresh and smelled like flowers.

"This way to the market, Mama!" Yasmin said, pointing at her map.

The street
was crowded.
There were people
everywhere!

"Hold my hand,
Yasmin. I don't want
you to get lost,"
Mama warned.

Their first
stop was the fruit
stall. Mama bought
strawberries and
bananas.

Yasmin sat down on the pavement and added the fruit stall to her map.

Their next stop was the bakery stall. It had all sorts of breads, and they all smelled delicious!

There were thin ones and fat ones. There were big ones and small ones. Yum!

"Two naan, please!" Mama called out.

Yasmin added the bakery stall to her map.

There were so many lovely smells and things to see. Yasmin saw a man holding balloons. Down the street a woman was selling roses. An ice-cream van was parked on the corner. Finally, she found what she was looking for. There was the playground! Yasmin was itching to explore.

"Mama, the park! I'll be right back!"

CHAPTER 3

A map to the rescue

Yasmin ran over to the swings. Swings were her favourite!

Up, up, up!

Then she went over to the sandpit. She would dig for buried treasure!

Yasmin was having so much
fun pretending. Then she thought
of something. Where was Mama?

Yasmin looked around, but
there were too many children.

Uh-oh.

Yasmin took a deep breath.
"I'm a brave explorer,"
she reminded
herself. "I can
find my way
back to Mama."

She still
had her map.
She unrolled it
and studied it.

She looked towards the man

with the balloons. Then the

woman selling roses and the

 ice-cream van. She saw the

fruit stall where Mama

had bought strawberries.

And she saw the bakery stall

where Mama had bought the

naan.

But no Mama.

Yasmin told herself not to cry.

Explorers don't cry.

Then she saw Mama's blue hijab. She ran towards her. "Mama!"

"There you are, Yasmin!" Mama said. "I was looking for you! You must tell me where you're going!"

"I did, but you didn't hear me. I'm sorry," Yasmin said, crying in relief.

"Let's go home and make dinner," Mama said and hugged Yasmin close. "Baba will be waiting for us."

Yasmin nodded. Next time she went exploring, she would take her map *and* Mama!

Think about it, talk about it

* Getting lost can be very scary.
  Think about what you would do
  if you got lost. Talk to your family
  and come up with a plan.

* If you could explore anywhere in
  the world, where would you go?
  What supplies would you take
  with you?

* Think about where you live. Are
  there houses and flats? Is there
  a park or a school or a shop
  nearby? Draw a map and show it
  to your family.

Learn Urdu with Yasmin!

Yasmin's family speaks both English and Urdu. Urdu is a language from Pakistan. You may already know some Urdu words!

baba father

hijab scarf covering the hair

jaan life; a sweet nickname for a loved one

kameez long tunic or shirt

mama mother

naan flatbread baked in the oven

nana grandfather on mother's side

nani grandmother on mother's side

sari dress worn by women in South Asia

Pakistan facts

Yasmin and her family are proud of their Pakistani culture. Yasmin loves to share facts about Pakistan!

Location

Pakistan is on the continent of Asia, with India on one side and Afghanistan on the other.

Islamabad

PAKISTAN

Currency

The currency (money) of Pakistan is called the rupee.

Language

The national language of Pakistan is Urdu, but English and several other languages are also spoken there.

(Salaam means Peace)

History

Independence Day in Pakistan is celebrated on 14 August.

A taste of Pakistan

Mango Lassi (Yogurt drink)

Ingredients:
- a few ice cubes
- 240 ml plain yogurt
- 120 ml water
- 2 teaspoons sugar
- 120 ml tinned mango pulp

What to do:
Crush the ice cubes in a blender. Add the yogurt, water, sugar and mango. Blend for about one minute. Serve cold.

Try this! If you don't have tinned mango, other crushed fruit is yummy too. Try peach or banana!

Saadia Faruqi is a Pakistani American writer, interfaith activist and cultural sensitivity trainer previously profiled in *O Magazine*. She is author of the adult short-story collection, *Brick Walls: Tales of Hope & Courage from Pakistan*. Her essays have been published in *Huffington Post*, *Upworthy* and *NBC Asian America*. She lives in Texas, USA, with her husband and children.

Hatem Aly is an Egyptian-born illustrator whose work has been featured in several publications worldwide. He currently lives in New Brunswick, Canada, with his wife, son and more pets than people. When he is not dipping cookies in a cup of tea or staring at blank pieces of paper, he is usually drawing books. One of the books he illustrated is *The Inquisitor's Tale* by Adam Gidwitz, which won a Newbery Honor and other awards, despite Hatem's drawings of a farting dragon, a two-headed cat and stinky cheese.

Join Yasmin
on all her adventures!

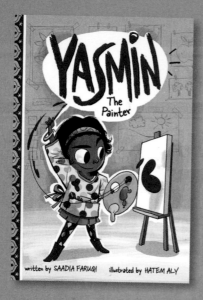

YASMIN
The Painter

written by SAADIA FARUQI   illustrated by HATEM ALY

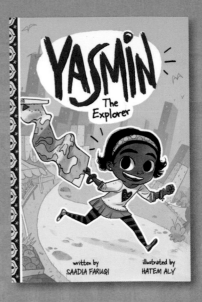

YASMIN
The Explorer

written by
SAADIA FARUQI   illustrated by
HATEM ALY

YASMIN
The Builder

written by SAADIA FARUQI   illustrated by HATEM ALY

YASMIN
The Fashion Model

written by SAADIA FARUQI   illustrated by HATEM ALY

Discover more at
www.raintree.co.uk